TO FOUR FUNNY HOTDOGS—
SUMMER, LEON, LUC AND XAVIER—A.D

TO MY LOVING WIFE, CLARE, AND MY
AWESOME PARENTS, ELAINE AND BILL—D.M

Text copyright © 2016 by Anh Do
Illustrations by Dan McGuiness

ISBN 978-1-338-58720-3
10 9 8 7 6 5 4 3 2 1   20 21 22 23 24
Printed in the U.S.A.   23
This edition first printing 2020
Typeset in YWFT Mullino.

ANH DO

ILLUSTRATED BY
DAN M^CGUINESS

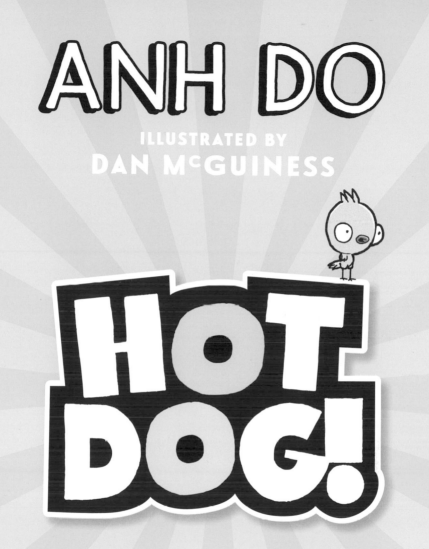

HOT DOG!

Scholastic Inc.

ONE

If you're thinking this book is about the yummy hot dog that you eat, then you're thinking of **the wrong hot dog!**

THIS thing will <u>NOT</u> be going on any adventures!

If you're thinking of the **super cute, super short, barking** type of hot dog ... then you've come to the right place!

I'm **Hotdog!** I'm a wiener dog, which means my legs are short, and I have a really L-o-o-o-n-g body.

Keep going.

There you go!

This morning I woke up with a **very stuffy nose.**

It was **so stuffy** I couldn't smell my breakfast!

I couldn't **smell** my toothpaste.

I couldn't even **smell** my feet!

But that's actually a pretty good thing. Feet never smell good!

Being a dog with very short legs is really good for lots of things, like playing hide-and-seek . . .

And **sleeping** . . .

Or dancing the **Limbo** . . .

But having short legs also makes it **hard** to do lots of things . . .
like **tying my shoelaces.**

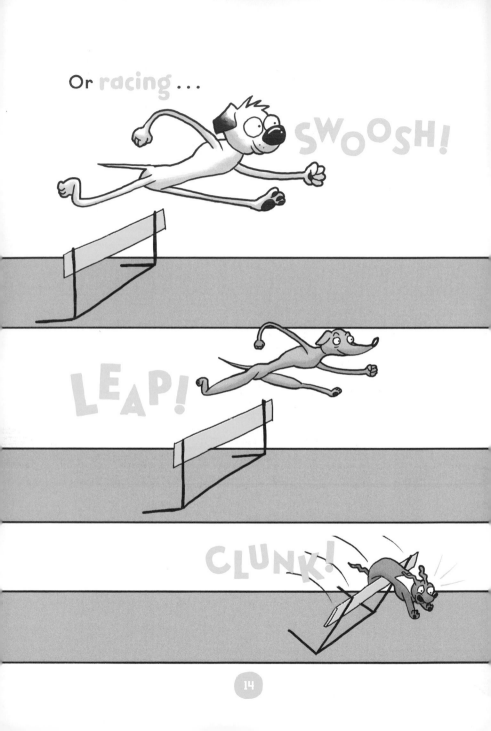

Or playing
guitar...

But that's okay, I usually figure out **another way** to do things.

That's the thing about me, I like to
keep on trying. No matter what!

And today, I was going to try and fly
my kite. Let's see if my friends
want to join in!

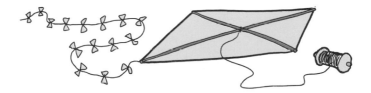

TWO

We were supposed to be meeting Lizzie right here by the big pine tree.

WHERE IS SHE?

Oh, there she is. "Oops, sorry, Lizzie."
Lizzie's a lizard who can blend in
with almost anything.

Or a **bunch of bananas**...

The worst is when she blends in with a
doorway.

We were both looking around the park, trying to see if Kevin was here yet. Kev's always last to show up . . .

All we could see was this weird-looking cow.

MOO!

Suddenly the cow wandered over.

"You guys, it's me, *Kevin*," said Kevin.

His humans must have dressed him up again. They love sticking him in crazy costumes!

Kevin dressed up as a shark.

Kevin dressed up as Santa.

Sometimes they even dress Kevin up as Kevin.

Kevin dressed up as Kevin.

Here's the thing you **need to know** about Kevin . . .

He is the **most relaxed animal** on earth.

Here's how his humans take him **for a walk.**

At home, he has a **grabbing tool** that he uses to reach things.

Like his **dinner bowl** ...

... or his **undies**.

He even has a *grabbing tool* he
uses to reach his *grabbing tool*.

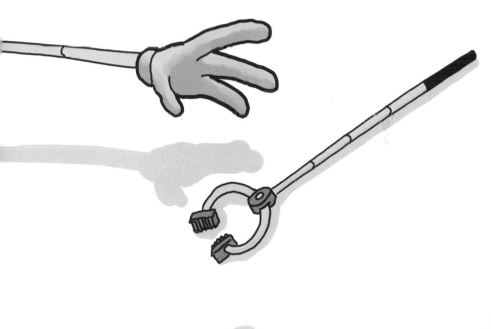

"That's a **really** bad outfit," said Lizzie.

"Go ahead and **laugh**," said Kev. "Just remember that cats are related to lions, the **king of the beasts**."

NOTHING WILL TAKE AWAY MY PRIDE!

As he said that, a yellow fluffy thing fell right on his head.

BONK!

WHAT WAS THAT?!

"Aw, look," said Lizzie, "it's a cute little bird. Poor little fella must have blown out of his nest."

Sure enough, there was an empty nest on a branch high above us.

"Now, off you go, bird, fly back to the tree," said Lizzie. "Flap those wings. Flap and flap, and fly through the sky!"

EEP!

What do we do now? I thought to myself. We can't leave this poor little guy without a way to get back to his nest.

We needed someone who could climb trees . . . and sausage dogs just don't climb trees.

"Kev!" I said. "You're a cat! Cats can climb stuff! Can you take him back up?"

DO I LOOK LIKE I'M DRESSED FOR CLIMBING?

No. I guess he had a point.

"Don't give me to the cat," said Birdy.
"He'll eat me!"

"Don't worry, Birdy," said Kev, "I'm more of a pie and fries and donut kind of guy. Plus I've had breakfast already."

We all turned to Lizzie.

You might be thinking . . . Yes, great idea, lizards can climb trees, right? Why doesn't the lizard take the baby bird back up?

Well . . . here's something you need to know about Lizzie.

She's one tough lizard. She can take on the biggest bully in the universe.

YOU WANT A PIECE OF ME? COME ON! MAKE IT SNAPPY!

She'll **eat anything**.
Even stuff Kev won't eat.

BIG BUG
BURGER

BUT when it comes to heights ...

she hates them! You won't find Lizzie
up a tree. Ever!

In fact, she even gets **dizzy** when she wears **high heels**!

"You know I'm **not** going up there,"
said Lizzie.

"Well, what do we do?" I asked. "We can't
just leave the baby bird here by himself . . ."

THREE

None of us could **figure out** a way to get the bird back up to his nest, so we decided to go and **find his mom.**

I was hoping to **fly my kite** today, but that would have to wait.

"So what does your mom **look like**?" I asked Birdy.

"I don't know," he said. "Like me, but **bigger**."

Normally I'd be able to use my nose to track down his mom, but it was still completely stuffy!

SNIFF!

Nothing!

"Hey, everyone!" Birdy suddenly shouted. "That's my mom over there!"

We all looked where Birdy was pointing. We saw just a tiny shape of another bird on the other side of the river, past the water park.

"Take me to her, Lizard Lady!" Birdy ordered.

"Quick!" I said. "Let's follow her!"

Problem was, between us and Birdy's mother was

a **BIG** river.

It wasn't like I could **doggie-paddle** across with everyone on my back . . .

A very BAD idea!

There was a **pair of oars** by the river, but **no boat** ... What could we do?

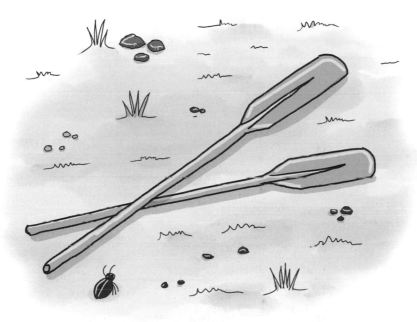

We needed something **strong**.

Something that would **float**.

We needed ...

"You're doing great, big guy!" I said.

"I hate water, Hotdog!" said Kev. "Don't you guys know cats hate water?"

"Kev, today you're a cow," said Lizzie. "Cows love water."

"Oh," said Kev. "Okay, then."

My arms might be little, but man, can they row! In no time we were almost halfway across the river.

We could almost see the other side when Kev started complaining about a REALLY bad smell.

My nose was still **blocked**, so I couldn't **smell** a thing!

"Kev, have you been **eating beans** again?" Kev had a bad bean habit, so I had to check it wasn't **him** he was smelling!

"No, I haven't had any beans!" he said.

So what was that terrible smell?

"It's . . . it's . . ." Kev began.

"It's—

POOP!"

shrieked Lizzie. "It's poop! The baby bird has pooped himself! I hate bird poop!"

EWWW!

"**Hey!**" Birdy cried. "You just need to change my diaper!"

"Oh, no," said Lizzie. "I didn't sign up for diaper changing. I'm a **poop-free zone.**"

"Please," begged Birdy. "It was just a little accident. I can't help that I'm still a baby!"

We were **wobbling** so much that Kev was about to tip over!

WHO**O**AA!

"Please, Lizzie, it's just **a tiny bit of bird poop**," I said. "We need your help!"

"Alright, alright!" said Lizzie. "I'll do it."

"Hey," I said, "where'd my **scarf** go?"

TA-DA!

"Now let's hurry up and find that bird."

FOUR

inally, we were on land again. "That was awesome, Kev," I said, patting my friend on the back. "Not only do you make a great cow, but you also make a great raft!"

At that moment we were interrupted by a whole bunch of—

QUACK!

QUACK!

"Hotdog!" said Lizzie. "We've found the mother! Hey you!" she yelled, reaching for the biggest duck.

The duck turned around. Lizzie took off the baby carrier and popped it on her.

"I believe this little birdy belongs to **you**."

QUACK?

"Lizard Lady, that's **not** my mom!" said Birdy.

"Yes, it is!" said Lizzie. "You've just been **apart** for so long that you've forgotten what she looks like."

"I know my own mom," said the baby bird.
"And this is **NOT** her."

"It's got **feathers**," said Lizzie. "It's got **wings**. It's **gotta be your mom**."

"You've got **Legs** and the cat's got **Legs**. That doesn't mean he's your mom," said Birdy.

The little guy **had a point!**

"Excuse me, duck," I said. "Is this baby bird yours?"

"I'm afraid not," she replied. "At least, I don't think I'm missing anyone."

1, 2, 3, 4, 5...

"I told you so," said the baby bird. "Hey, there's my mom over there! She's heading down that path!"

Again, we all looked up for Birdy's mom. I saw a flash of feathers flying down toward a big barn.

She was headed for the **berry farm**!

"Let's go!"

FIVE

We reached the **farm** and stood by the gates, wondering how in the world we were going to get **inside**. We needed a **pig**, or a **horse**, or a **sheep**, or a . . .

FARM ANIMALS
ONLY

And it wasn't long before he came back!

LOOK! I FOUND YOUR MOM!

"That's not my mom!" said Birdy.

"Huh?" said Kev. "Are you sure? It has to be!"

"Here we go again," said Birdy. "I know what my mom looks like, and that hen is not her! Not even close! My mom looks much less . . . like him."

"I'm not a hen, thanks very much. I'm a rooster," said the rooster. "I'm a karate-chopping rooster!"

That rooster was one
really tough guy!

"We're never going to find her," said Birdy. "Eep, eep, eep," he sobbed.

"Of course we will," said Lizzie. "Look at this amazing team that's on the case. What could possibly go wrong?"

Just then I saw another **flash of feathers** in the sky.

"Wait a minute," I said. "Is that her up there?"

MAMA!

She was heading toward the **beach**!

"Come on, guys, let's go!"

SIX

"That's **my mom** up there!" said Birdy. He was pointing all the way up to the **lighthouse**.

I could just see the bird right next to the lighthouse window.

I looked at my friends. We were all **exhausted**.

Poor Kev.

Lizzie looked **tired**, too. She'd been carrying Birdy around **all day**!

We'd **never** make it up the lighthouse stairs in time to catch the mother.

So how could we make it there **faster**?

We needed a **helicopter** or a **hot-air balloon** . . . or . . . or . . .

a kite!

HEEEEELLLLLLLLLLP...

A great gust of wind sent us soaring
up to the lighthouse. It was awesome!

"So this is what it's like to **fly**!" said Birdy.

"Get ready to drop!" I called out to everyone as we neared the top of the lighthouse.

"Ready, set . . ."

We landed with a **loud splat!**

I was **untangling** myself from my kite when I heard Lizzie **cry** out.

"**FINALLY!**" she said. "We **found** your mom, Birdy!"

I turned around.

YOUR MOM!

"She's **not** my mom!" Birdy shouted. "You really don't know much about birds, do you?"

"No, no, you're just confused because your mom is wearing this **funny dinner jacket**," said Lizzie.

"It's not a jacket, I'm a penguin," said the penguin. "And I am **not** that baby's mother."

"And what's a penguin doing all the way up here?" said Lizzie.

"What does it look like I'm doing?" said the penguin. "I'm up here for the **photos**!"

SAY CHEESE!

We must have frightened Birdy's real mom away, because there was no one else around aside from a **busload** of **penguins**.

Slowly, we made our way back down the stairs to the beach.

Birdy was looking **really sad**.

We'd come so close to Birdy's mom three times. I normally solved problems, but I was running **out of ideas!**

I MISS MY MOM . . .

Lizzie looked really tired.

"Lizzie, want me to take him for a little while?" I asked.

"Yes, please. Thanks, Hotdog."

I took the baby sling. As I picked Birdy up, his little head feathers tickled my nose.

A—

The **enormous** sneeze completely **unblocked** my nose. I could **smell** again!

"I can smell the **sea**, I can smell **fish-and-chips . . .**

But best of all, I can smell **pine and berries** and the **river**! And I'm sure that's the smell of **Birdy's mom**!"

I followed my nose away from the
beach . . . where we'd flown the kite.

Past the berries and the farm . . .
Around the river . . . and all the way
back to the big pine tree, where
our adventure began.

Suddenly, over at the water park, I saw something that looked just like Birdy, but bigger! It must have been Birdy's mom!

She was perched on top of the mini waterslide!

It was a long tube that went around and waaaay up high.

I looked over at the stairs to the top, but the gate was bolted shut.

We had to find someone who could climb up that tube. It was not going to be easy.

We needed someone who would try their hardest to make it. Someone who wouldn't give up. Someone like me!

"Okay, Birdy," I said, "I'm going to get you to your mom!"

HERE WE GO!

It was **REALLY** tricky getting up the slide!

There were lots of tough *twists* and *turns*.

But we finally made it to the top. **Phew!**

Just as I was about to climb out of the slide, Birdy's mom flew off again! **Can you believe it?!**

But I still wasn't going to give up! This was our chance! We had to **keep trying!**

I climbed out as **fast** as I could, and then we both yelled with all our might!

MOOOMMYY!!!

And guess what? She must have heard us because she turned around!

YAY!

I was so tired, I leaned back and **slipped**!

Birdy and I slid all the way back down the slide!

Lizzie and Kev **helped** us
out of the water.

MAMA!

"I've been **Looking for you everywhere**," said the bird. "What happened to you?"

The bird turned to me and Lizzie and Kev. She looked very confused.

"A big gust of wind **blew me** out of the nest," said Birdy.

"He can't fly yet," said Lizzie, "so he was **stuck** on the ground."

"All by himself," I added.

"So we went looking for you," I explained. "To get him back to you."

"Mama! I missed you so much!" said Winston. "These are my new friends, and we had the BEST DAY EVER!"

THE BEST DAY EVER?

"We went **rafting**," he said, "we went to the **farm**, we **flew a kite**! We had so much **fun**!"

"I think this calls for a **celebration**," said Kev.

"Well, you did return Winston to me safe and sound. I think I owe you a party," said Mama Bird.

"With cake?" said Kev.

What a day!

We found Winston's mom, flew a kite, and even made some new friends. I can't wait for our **next adventure!**

MORE ADVENTURES COMING SOON!